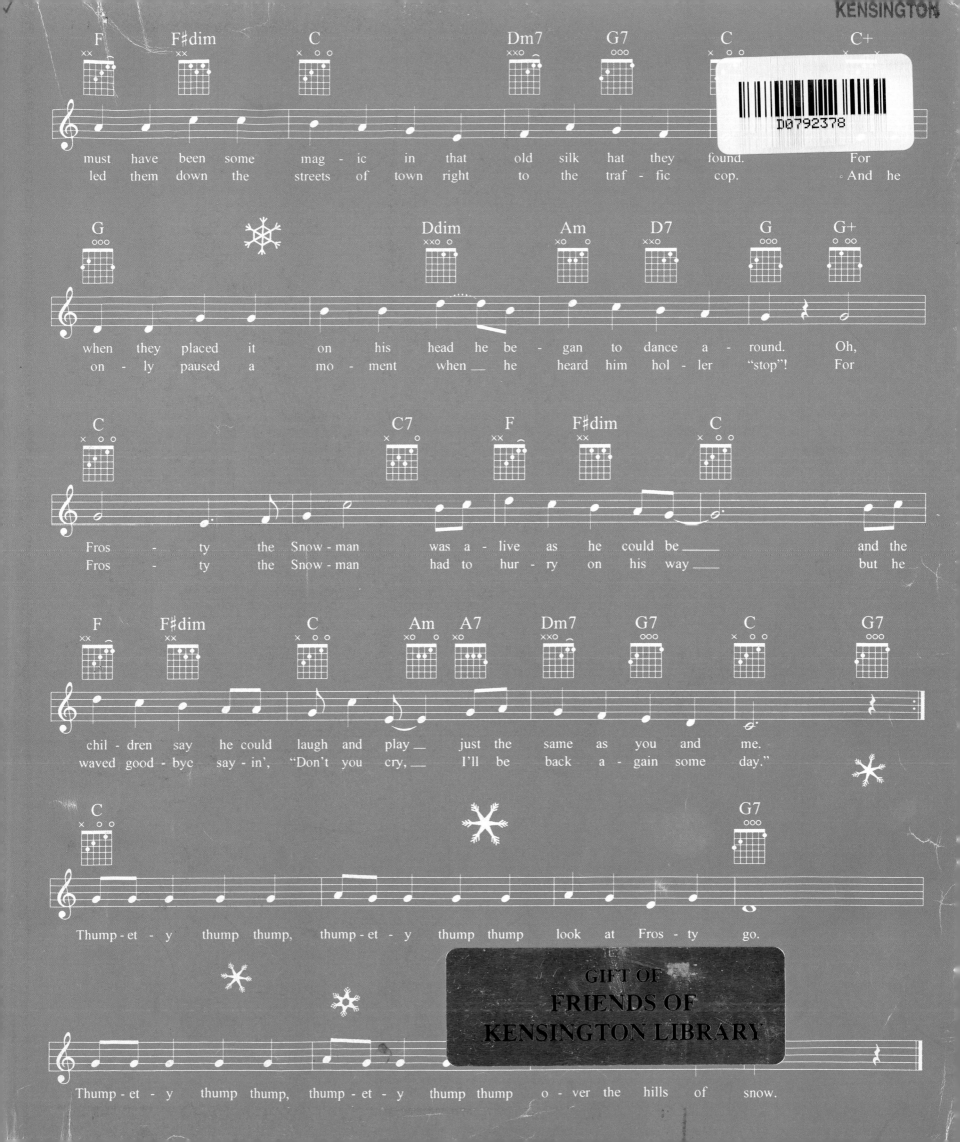

Frosty the Snowman

By Steve Nelson and Jack Rollins
Illustrated by Richard Cowdrey

Dedicated to Maddie, Joel, and those to come . . . .
Soli Deo Gloria!—R.C.

Grosset & Dunlap ❄ New York

Based upon the musical composition FROSTY THE SNOWMAN. FROSTY THE SNOWMAN, characters, names and all related indicia are trademarks of and © Warner/Chappell Music, Inc. (s03) All rights reserved. Published by Grosset & Dunlap, a division of Penguin Young Readers Group, 345 Hudson Street, New York, NY 10014. GROSSET & DUNLAP is a trademark of Penguin Group (USA) Inc. Published simultaneously in Canada. Printed in the U.S.A.

Library of Congress Cataloging-in-Publication Data is available.

ISBN 0-448-43199-8   A B C D E F G H I J

Frosty the Snowman was a jolly, happy soul,
with a corncob pipe
and a button nose
and two eyes made out of coal.

Frosty the Snowman is a fairy tale they say,
he was made of snow
but the children know
how he came to life one day.

There must have been
some magic
in that old silk hat
they found.

For when they placed it on his head,

he began to dance around!

Oh, Frosty the Snowman
was alive as he could be,
and the children say
he could laugh and play

just the same as
you and me.

**Frosty the Snowman
knew the sun was hot that day,**

So he said,
"Let's run
and we'll have
some fun

now before I melt away!"

Down to the village,
with a broomstick in his hand,
running here and there
all around the square,
saying, "Catch me if you can!"

He led them down the streets of town
right to the traffic cop.
And he only paused a moment
when he heard him holler,

"Stop!"

For Frosty the Snowman had to hurry on his way
but he waved good-bye,
saying, "Don't you cry,
I'll be back again some day."

Thumpety thump thump,
thumpety thump thump,
look at Frosty go.

Thumpety thump thump,
thumpety thump thump,
over the hills of snow!

FROSTY THE SNOWMAN

Words and Music by
STEVE NELSON and
JACK ROLLINS

Moderately

mf

rit.

C   C7   F   F♯dim   C

1. Fros - ty, the Snow - man was a jol - ly hap - py soul, ___ with a
2. Fros - ty, the Snow - man knew the sun was hot that day, ___ so he

F   F♯dim   C   A7   Dm7   G7   C   G7

corn cob pipe and a but - ton nose ___ and two eyes made out of coal.
said "Let's run and we'll have some fun ___ now be - fore I melt a - way."

C   C7   F   F♯dim   C

Fros - ty the Snow - man is a fair - y tale they say, ___ he was
Down to the vil - lage with a broom - stick in his hand, ___ run - ning

F   F♯dim   C   Am   A7   Dm7   G7   C   C7

made of snow but the chil - dren know ___ how he came to life one day. There
here and there all a - round the square, ___ say - in' "catch me if you can." He